ALSO BY NATASHA LUXE

Celebrity Crush Series

PLOT TWIST
OFF CAMERA

The *Heroes and Villains* Series with Liza Penn:

NEMESIS
ALTER EGO
SECRET SANCTUM
MAGICIAN
THUNDER
GODDESS

Never miss a sexy release!
Join my mailing list:

https://rarebooks.substack.com/welcome

A Celebrity Crush Story

MEET
cute

BESTSELLING AUTHOR
Natasha Luxe

CHAPTER ONE:
TOM

Havensboro definitely lives up to its reputation.

The producer of *Run Aground* had been calling this tiny Maine island *idyllic* from the moment he pitched his film to me. My manager reiterated it, adding *quaint*. My agent doubled down with *tranquil*.

Is it really that obvious that I need a break?

Though if they were that concerned with my mental wellbeing, none of them would be pushing me to do this role quite so hard, so their concern is kind of half-assed.

Still. The moment I step off the ferry and clomp down the dock towards the main street—literally the main, as in only, street—I feel a weight lift off my shoulders. Maybe it's the salt-tinged air. Maybe it's the crash and murmur of waves, ceaseless, relentless, better than any manufactured sound machine.

Something about this island is downright peaceful, and I immediately fall in love.

I shake my head and heft my duffel bag higher up my shoulder. Stupid to get attached to anything, be it place or person. The job comes first. Always.

A light rain starts to drizzle, and I pull the collar of my wool coat higher as I head across the ferry parking lot. Luckily, the shitty weather makes everyone angle quickly for shelter, so no one pays much attention to me—but I imagine in a place like this, something as novel as a newcomer will cause a lot of chaos. Not that it's anything I'm not used to, but damn, it feels nice to have the expected attention be just small-town curiosity and not raving paparazzi.

The building first off the parking lot is a Victorian-style house with a sign out front saying it's the Havensboro Inn. An actual white picket fence rims the place, and when I push through the gate, I'm greeted by plump green bushes and pink and purple flowers lining a stone walkway to the sprawling wrap around porch.

Definitely not something you'd see in LA, unless it was on a movie set.

I jog up the steps, note a garden gnome standing vigil—he's wearing a kilt, good man—and shove inside.

A bell rings above me. The entryway is dominated by a massive mahogany staircase that shoots up to the second floor, the walls done in deep, rich scarlets and browns to create a homey atmosphere. The air smells of baked goods—something vanilla, maybe cinnamon? Whatever it is, my stomach grumbles, my shoulders relax, and I think for possibly the hundredth time what a good idea it was to come to Havensboro before production set up.

This is the true town. The town we'll be embodying in *Run Aground*. This authentic feel will evaporate the moment the crew plods onto the island, so it's up to me to soak in all I can and then give it right back to the camera during filming.

Quaint. Idyllic. But resilient too, an island that's withstood centuries of Atlantic Ocean battering, marauding pirates, various wars. It's a survivor, but that survival has manifested in a calm, unhurried energy that's way too addicting.

A throat clears.

I've been staring into space, drumming the fingers of my left hand against my thigh in what the press calls *the Tom Hudel Tap*. I'd

—

tried to stop once the tabloids caught onto my nervous habit, but my agent loved it, told me to keep on doing anything that made me seem *real* and *approachable*.

Because without this nervous tic, I'd be an off-putting monster, apparently?

I turn to see a desk off to the side. A squat old woman sits on a stool. She stares at me with cold, narrow eyes and I fight the urge to duck my head.

My mind instantly places her. She'd shine as an oppressive Catholic schoolteacher, or the disapproving mother-in-law, or really any of the grab bag of old crone archetypes.

I wince, but I can't help it. Analyzing people based on characterizations is an unfortunate side effect of the acting gig. The world is a story, all of us mere players, eh?

"Name?" she asks, distrust ripe in her tone.

"Uh—Thomas. Thomas Smith." It's better to lie for now. The whole point of coming here early was to lay low, soak up the *real* Havensboro. I can't control whether someone recognizes me eventually, but for now, I can keep my presence on the downlow.

"Hm," the woman responds like she can tell I'm lying. "Would you like a room? Two-fifty a night."

"Yes," I say.

"*Two-fifty*. Per night."

"I—yes, I heard you." Do I look cheap? I'd tried to tone down the LA fashion—a wool coat, black jeans, simple shoes. I even scaled back the product in my hair and just tied my shoulder-length curls into a knot at the back of my head. But I know I don't look hard pressed for money.

She blinks at me, disbelieving, and I realize she's just chosen to hate me.

It makes me like her. She's really committing to the role, in a way.

I turn on the charm and add, with a dimpled smile, "Please."

Her eyebrows lift. But overall, her attitude doesn't change in the least.

She flips open a ledger and starts writing my name next to a room number. "Length of stay?"

"A week." Once the crew shows up, I'll be bunking off the island and ferrying over as needed.

"Hm," she says again. She passes me an iron key. No plastic scanner cards; no electronic fobs.

Fuck, I love this place. It's like traveling back in time.

My joy must be pretty evident on my face because the woman narrows her eyes even more.

"Reason for your stay?" she asks.

I hesitate, hand extended from taking the key. "Is that necessary?"

She gives me a flat stare.

"I'm part of the movie crew coming in a few days," I relent. "I was sent early to get the lay of the land."

I may as well have said I was a drug lord hoping to set up shop.

The woman growls at me. Actually *growls*. "The mayor might be overjoyed for this little publicity stunt, but Havensboro doesn't *need* your type here. So you keep to yourself, you hear? You leave this island exactly as you found it, or you'll deal with me personally."

"We aren't planning to construct anything if that's what you mean. We'll treat this island with respect."

"Hm." There's that harumph again. Critics would call it *overkill* at this point, but I think it feels true to her. She bats her hand at the stairs. "Room 211. Breakfast is served at 5:30. Kitchen closes at 7."

"*A.M.?*" Shit—it's only 9 right now. I'd hoped, by the smell, that there'd be something in the way of food.

Wrong answer.

The woman's nostrils flare.

"I mean—5:30 is fine," I add.

The woman drops her glare to the ledger. I linger for a beat, only to get another impatient wave toward the stairs.

I grin at her. "Thank you, madame. You run a truly charming establishment."

And I mean it. Rudeness and all. We *are* invading this private little island, so I get the attitude. But aside from that, this place is clearly nice, and clearly well cared for.

The woman cuts me a look. Does her anger soften a bit? I smile again and make for the stairs.

"Oh." I swing back. "Is there, by chance, somewhere around here serving breakfast still?"

She scribbles in her ledger. "Diner across the road is open 24-hours."

"Thank you, madame," I say again, touching my forehead where a hat brim would be.

She rolls her eyes.

Ah, I'm getting to her.

Up the stairs I go and find a room exactly like what I'd expected. A four-poster bed done up in frilly linens and a half dozen throw pillows. A tiny bathroom with an ancient tub and wrap-around shower curtain. An armoire with extra blankets that smell of vanilla and lavender.

I unpack, freshen up, and head back downstairs, and it takes a great deal of restraint not to badger the poor proprietor into talking to me again. I want to know everything about this island. The history, the *real* history, not just the watered-down story we'll be filming. There's a sort of magic here, an endurance that's electrifying.

But I leave the woman be and slip out into the rain.

The diner is indeed directly across the street, sharing the far edge of the ferry's parking lot. A few cars are parked there, and I can see other patrons within.

I push inside. Nothing fancy, but the place has the same entrancing energy as the inn, as this island overall. A twist of *fate*, almost.

I'm supposed to be here. I can feel it in the pit of my stomach.

A sign says *Seat Yourself,* so I shrug out of my coat, hook it on the wrack by the door, and take a booth at the very back, giving me a good view of the place. There's a bar that runs the length of the room and a waitress slides plates from the window to the customers seated there, talking animatedly to people who must be regulars.

Another waitress is at the far end of the long diner, taking an order from a family of four in a corner booth.

My eyes snag on her, drawn by some invisible pull. I feel it the same way I could feel my growing tie to this island. *I'm supposed to be here. Fate.*

She's bent over the booth, and whatever she says sets off the toddler boy in a fit of giggles.

My mouth curves in a half smile—until she shifts, and I get a nice view of her ass. Firm and high, with long, smooth legs, one of which pops out to balance herself.

My dick hardens.

Damn, stop; this is a family place.

I grab a menu that shows basic diner fare, though far from what I normally eat. Carbs galore. Hardly a vegetable in sight. But also tons of seafood, lobster omelets and crab cake benedict, and—ah, heaven, a whole page of pancakes—

"What can I get you to drink?"

The voice is airy, delicate, with the faintest whisp at the back of her throat that instantly has me imagining her moaning.

Get a grip—
I look up.
And all grip is gone.

The second waitress stands at my booth. My brain does its usual calculations, trying to place her in a script, but there's only one role, one possible outcome: leading lady, main character, the gravitational heart of any story.

She has a pad and pen held waiting in thin, delicate fingers, her nails painted purple. Her bright blue eyes are wide and welcoming, and her tongue quickly darts out, wetting her glossy red lips, an unconscious move that has my dick throbbing. She tips her head, spilling soft brown curls over her shoulder, leading my eyes down to the overall shorts she's wearing on top of a pink tank top. One of the straps is popped open, flapping against her stomach, showing her rounded breast and the faintest outline of a lacy bra through the thin tank top. The shorts stop mid-thigh, wrapping tight around her smooth skin, and there's a birthmark just there, peeking out from under the hem.

My mouth waters. She shifts and the flap of her overalls bounces, and I'm hit with the sudden image of using that material to haul her onto this table and finding out what that birthmark tastes like.

Good god, what is wrong with me? I've seen attractive women before. Hell, I'm an actor; I've screen-fucked some of the hottest women in the world. But *this* woman is on a whole other level, that perfect mix of small-town innocence and easy sexiness, like she knows that what she has to offer is on par with godliness.

"Coffee," I manage. "With…"

Oh shit, am I self-conscious? What the fuck.

The downright sexy confidence pouring off this woman has me feeling not like my usual leading man, but some background extra, a drooling schoolboy or Diner Patron #2.

Jesus Christ, I have an Oscar. Again I say, *what the fuck.*

"With?" she prods, grinning.

Did she clock me checking her out? It makes my dick even harder.

I shift, trying to subtly adjust through my tight jeans. It's distracting enough that I say the rest of my order, something totally indulgent because there's no one here to give me disapproving *is that a CARB* eyes. "With some vanilla syrup if you have it. Or some chocolate syrup too. And whipped cream."

The woman arches one eyebrow. Fuck, it's sexy, a perfect curve over her glittering eyes.

"Got a sweet tooth, huh?" she asks.

"Oh," I say, my voice deepening, "you have no idea."

She laughs. It's as light as her voice, tinkling with joy. I can't help but smile too, drawn into her reaction like a moth to a flame.

My smile elicits the usual response. The woman blushes, the most delicious shade of pink tinting her cheeks and creeping down her neck to the beginning swells of her cleavage. A little more of my control returns, the blood rushing back up to my head, though my cock stays hard.

Especially when she leans one hip on the edge of the booth across from me, and her overalls pull even tighter against the flat plane of her stomach. Is she wearing underwear? That outfit is such a tease, innocent but so very *not*.

I splay my hands on my knees under the table. Grip them into fists. Again.

She writes my order on her pad. "I'll be back with it." She gives me another smile. "Name's Avery."

"Tom. Thanks. Avery," I say her name after a pause, with intention, enjoying the curve of the letters on my tongue.

And then she *bites her fucking lip*.

I almost blow right then.

A voice in my head tells me that I'm here to experience Havensboro, so I might as well *experience Havensboro*.

But I put the brakes on that thought *really* fast. One, because I've never been good at the one night stand scene; and two, because this woman deserves better than that. I meant what I said to the innkeeper—we'll treat this island with respect. *I* will treat this island with respect. I didn't become an actor for the glitz and fucking side of things; I became an actor for the *acting* side of things, the bliss of losing myself over to a role, of uncovering facets of a character and portraying them on screen in a way that will connect with audiences all over the world.

But it does get damn lonely. Because even if I did ask her out, I'd be back in LA in a few weeks, then off to the next shoot location. What do I really have to offer?

There's a reason very few relationships last in Hollywood. I know where my priorities are.

She turns, walking for the bar, and my eyes plant right on her ass.

Well. I know where my priorities *want* to be.

CHAPTER TWO: AVERY

Hollywood has come to Havensboro.

And, god help me, it's sexy as hell, with the lightest British accent and smelling of expensive spicy cologne.

I shimmy behind the bar. Gwen's already halfway to me, darting past Kevin at his usual stool, who lifts his mug.

"Refill, sweetheart."

"In a sec, Kev."

"But I—"

"*In a second, Kevin.*" Gwen blatantly ignores her husband and grabs my arm as I turn to the coffee pots.

Her nails pinch into me. "*Who the fuck is that?*" she hiss-squeals into my ear.

I shrug. But my skin still feels hot, and I know the blush is staining my chest. I always was the worst when it came to hiding being flustered. "Said his name was Tom."

He looks familiar, but I can't imagine I've seen someone involved in LA movie production before. He must just have one of those faces.

"Producer, you think?" Gwen sneaks a look over my shoulder as I fill a mug with coffee.

"Maybe. Makes sense."

"They're not due to start shooting for another week!"

"They need to set up, right?"

"I guess." Gwen stares openly at the man. Tom. She sighs and pulls the collar of her shirt, fanning herself. "Now I see why Mayor Johnson agreed to this film. One look at that guy and I've basically come."

"Gwen!" I giggle at her and add a squirt of vanilla syrup to the coffee. Another. One more for good measure. Then I grab a whipped cream canister and pile on a mountain of it.

Sweet tooth, huh?

Oh, you have no idea.

I glance to the side.

Tom is watching me. His eyes don't even flicker, no hint of the nervousness he'd briefly shown. His sumptuous lips curve into a small smile, something private, like we're sharing a secret.

My body heats again. I feel that heat everywhere, spreading down my breasts, my piqued nipples, my stomach, my wet slit. God, I'm dripping already. Has it just been too long since I've gotten any, or is Tom *that* hot?

He leans back in the booth and pulls out a phone. The moment his attention falls from me, I keep right on raking my eyes over him. He's built, that's for sure. Long, lean muscles, the kind only someone with time and money can achieve, each sinew perfectly sculpted. He's in a tight long sleeved black shirt that shows off every cut and curve, matching the black skinny jeans and dark shoes. All that black could be depressing, but on him it looks like he's some kind of starving poet fresh off a Parisian tour. His brown hair has a curl to it, the strands that are loose around his face at least; the rest is pulled back behind his head, showing a jaw so sharp it could saw the clothes right off my body.

God, yep, it *has* been too long since I've gotten any. There aren't exactly a lot of choices on Havensboro—my ex-boyfriend ended up marrying my best friend, and it only took about a month to rotate through the remaining eligible Havensboro bachelors.

Which is reason number one I'll be out of here in just $200 more dollars.

"Whoever he is," I say to Gwen, "let's hope he's a good tipper."

But Gwen's finally giving her husband—my ex—more coffee. Kevin follows her gaze to Tom before elbowing his friends.

It won't be long before the whole island knows Tom is here, and someone's dug into his past to figure out exactly what part he plays in this upcoming movie.

That's reason number two I'm leaving. Everyone's business is *everyone's business*, and just once, I'd like to go somewhere where no one knows every single dirty piece of my life.

$200 more dollars, and I'll have exactly what I need to get a down payment on an apartment in Boston, along with two months of rent while I find a job.

Havensboro may have attracted a fancy movie producer with its promises of peace and quiet, but I'd give anything for loud. Messy. Chaotic.

Hot. Throbbing.

My hands are sweaty. I scrape them on my overalls, the material dragging across my sensitive nipples, and I hiss a breath as I pick up Tom's drink.

The moment I come out from behind the bar, his eyes are back on me. There's a deeper twist in the way he watches me, like he's trying to place something—if he's seen me somewhere, maybe, or if he's trying to figure me out. Whatever the reason, I have fun swaying my hips a little as I put his coffee in front of him.

A dollop of whipped cream drips off the quickly melting pile, landing on my thumb.

I can't help it. I really can't.

I lift my thumb and stick the whole thing into my mouth, slowly pulling it out, the cream soft and sweet.

Tom's eyes go wide. I hear him hiss "Jesus Christ," under his breath.

My clit throbs and I fight a smile.

"What can I get you to eat?" I ask.

"Eat?" he echoes.

"Yes. Food?"

"Ah."

Is he blushing? Shit, that's cute—no, it's *sexy*. He exudes confidence, but I seem very easily able to make him trip.

"How about the…" He points to the menu.

I lean over. And grin. "You really do like sugar."

His eyes are on my cleavage. I hadn't even intended that.

I go still, realizing how close we are. The air between us is charged and scorching, tinged with that spicy cologne he's wearing and a bit of vanilla from the whipped cream melting nearby.

He meets my eyes, his voice low. "Homemade chocolate chip pancakes—who could resist that?"

"Fair enough," I manage. "With syrup and whipped cream too?"

He blushes again.

God help me.

I pull back, just to be able to fucking *breathe,* and write his order down. "It'll be out shortly."

I have no reason to stay talking to him, but I want to, so I turn more slowly than normal, my teeth digging into my lip again.

"Wait."

I spin back around. "Yeah?"

His hand taps out a rhythm on his thigh under the table. "I, um—I'm here to do some research on the island," he says. "I was wondering if you knew who I should speak with? Town historian, someone with the longest knowledge—"

"Ah." I slide into the booth across from him. He sips in a breath. "That'd be Clarice McDermott. She runs the Havensboro Museum."

"Excellent. Where can I find her?"

I point out the window. "She also manages the Havensboro Inn. The museum's attached to it."

Tom's face falls. But he brings up a laugh. "That could pose a problem. The proprietor does not seem exactly…taken…with my presence."

My grin widens. "Clarice isn't taken with *anyone's* presence. I wore a dress that didn't quite go to my fingertips for tenth grade homecoming, and she's never forgiven me."

He tips his head. "Oh?"

The way he says that makes me think he's imagining me in that dress. One not that much shorter than my current overalls.

I shift on the bench and my ankle bumps something soft, warm.

Tom's legs.

I freeze. His eyes widen slightly, the pupils dilating.

He doesn't pull away.

The pickings are *way* too slim here on Havensboro. I knew the movie would bring in a new crowd, but it honestly hadn't occurred to me until this moment that it might bring in someone…interesting. Someone oozing sexuality in such a potent way that I'm on the edge of orgasm with just my ankle touching his leg.

Daring, maybe *too* daring, I slip off my ballet flat.

And slowly run my foot up his calf.

"Is there—ah—" He blinks quickly and shifts in his seat as my foot creeps higher. "Is there anyone else I could speak with? About the island?"

"Pretty much anyone who lives here," I say. My foot reaches his knee; he's tapping on it again, and when I try to press higher, those fingers snatch my ankle.

My breath catches. I expect him to shove my foot down and put a stop to this, but he lets his fingers drape loose around my skin, a delicate brush as he runs his touch across the top of my foot, back down.

Shivers dance up my body.

He wraps his fingers in a firm grip around my ankle and lifts my foot over his knee until it rests against his crotch.

I can feel his hard-on straining against his jeans. The waves of shivers shoot straight to my wet slit, tingles and heat spreading down my thighs and up my stomach.

We hold each other's eyes, both daring the other to stop.

Fuck, we don't even know one another.

And that's what makes it so exciting.

I'll be off Havensboro in just a few more weeks—less if the movie brings in enough business to boost my tips. Whoever this guy is will likewise be gone the moment the movie's done.

Knowing this is temporary before it's even begun sends a little thrill through me. A hot fling could be exactly what I need right now. Clear my mind, get me to focus on these last few pushes of hard work before I leave Havensboro for bigger horizons.

I rub my foot down the considerable length of his cock. Holy *shit*—he's huge. My pussy aches and I practically whimper.

Tom rocks forward, pushing against my foot, but then he smiles at me, a lopsided, cocky grin that makes his handsome face even more irresistible, and he knows it.

His fingers creep up my ankle and swirl circles on my calf. "You wouldn't be interested in being my Havensboro tour guide, would you, Avery?"

God, say my name again. "I'm off in an hour."

CHAPTER THREE: TOM

There are a hundred reasons why this is a bad idea, but not a one of them stops me from lingering in that booth for the next hour.

I watch Avery flit around the diner, her movements graceful and sure. She balances trays with ease. Every customer gets an honest smile—though none of her smiles are the same she'd given me, sultry and teasing. My gaze catches her attention often, and she blushes and winks at me, and my god, I'm in trouble.

She's going to help me get to know the real Havensboro. That's all.

But my crotch is still warm from her toes on my dick. Did I imagine all that? She didn't even seem to recognize me—none of that flirting was the usual display of a someone throwing themselves at me. She seemed actually...interested. In me.

I finish my pancakes and count the minutes down until, finally, Avery comes over to me.

"I'm off," she says as she pulls on a thin raincoat. "Ready?"

Hell yes. "Let's go."

I toss a stack of money onto the table, then rethink it and just hand it all to her. "I forgot to pay. And here's your tip."

Avery takes the money, counts it, and her eyebrows shoot up.

"I threw in a little extra for your assistance with my Havensboro research."

"How do you know I'll even be of any help?"

I smile. "Call it a gut instinct."

She bites her lip in that cock-hardening way and I'm tempted to shove even more money at her. But a pulse of horror rocks through me—she doesn't think I'm *paying* her to…for…oh shit.

"Not that I—" I clear my throat. "I really do need assistance with my research. You may have guessed, but it's for the movie."

"Ah." She smiles as she leads me to the door.

I slip on my coat and catch the other waitress giving Avery an enthusiastic thumbs up.

Avery rolls her eyes and pushes the door open with her hip.

"So what's your role in the film?" she asks.

She doesn't recognize me. My chest swells with a rare burst of freedom.

"Authenticity," I say. It isn't exactly a lie, but I still feel guilty as we duck out into the drizzle. She's kind enough to help me—and flirt pretty heavily with me—the least I can do is be honest about who I am.

But it's too tempting to just be…*me*. For a little while.

I offer her my arm as we cross the parking lot. Avery gives me an odd look, like she's not used to guys doing stuff like that, before she tucks her hand in the crook of my elbow.

The weight of her fingers sears through my coat's sleeve. She pulls her body close to mine, shivering a little—she has to be freezing in this rain, wearing only a coat and those overall shorts.

Not on my watch.

I untangle our arms, open the side of my coat, and tuck her up against me, wrapping my arm around her, pulling her into my warmth. She folds in with a contented sigh.

"Thanks," she says and blinks up at me, a droplet of rain on her eyelashes.

We're nearly back to the inn. I both want to get her inside, out of this rain, and never want this moment to end. The way she's looking at me sets off that fire again, the electric tension that has my cock straining for release. I've never been this turned on by such innocent touches before.

The Havensboro Inn's door chimes over us, but thankfully, Ms. McDermott is nowhere in sight.

"The museum's back here," Avery says, shrugging out of her raincoat. She hangs it up and I do the same. The drizzle has flattened her hair and she shakes her fingers through the long strands, perfuming the air with hints of mango scented shampoo.

Fuck. I stagger, instinctually following that smell closer towards her.

She doesn't back away.

"Uh, back there, you said?" I clarify, pointing off into the house, my voice gruff.

She hooks her thumbs into the sides of her overalls. "Yeah. We should…be the only ones there. It's more a pet project of Clarice's than any real tourist draw."

"Hm." The moan is the only noise I can make.

One word beats in my head.

Alone.

We'll be alone in there.

Avery turns, and the way she pulls on her overalls gives me a brief flash down inside, of her stomach covered in that pink tank top, and lower, is that a tuft of hair?

She isn't wearing panties.

Fuck, fuck, *fuck*.

I follow her. I'm helpless not to.

She leads me through the inn to a door off the back. A plaque on the outside says *Havensboro Museum.*

Inside is a small room with low lighting to focus on the spotlights that illuminate various pedestals and objects. The world's smallest museum.

Half my brain starts to shake awake. This is exactly what I need—I see antique books and manuscripts, pictures and memorabilia, all things that will help me get to the bottom of the character I'll be portraying. I've done what research I can on my own, of course, but these items, this history—it's a gold mine

The door swings shut behind me and I go to the first display. It's a glass case covering an old logbook from a shipping vessel.

"The movie's about Captain Small, right?" Avery asks. She stands a few feet from me, her eyes idly casting over the relics—this must be pretty boring for her, actually. How often has she seen this museum?

"Yes." I squint, trying to make out the writing on the logbook. Maybe Ms. McDermott could be convinced to remove the glass case for me? Unlikely. The plaque on the pedestal says it is indeed Captain Small's—it's a good guess most of the relics in here are his. Havensboro's proudest son.

"The story of his June 1818 voyage," I continue. I move to the next display case, closer to Avery, who stays where she is. "How he beat the storm to return home."

Avery cocks her head. "That's it?"

I straighten from where I'd been looking at an old compass. "Yes?"

She frowns at me and moves to the side, showing the display case she'd been in front of. I bend closer.

It's a whole box full of letters, a pair of delicate silk gloves, a pearl necklace. The plaque says *Maria Small*.

"His wife is in the script," I say. "He returns to home to her, and—"

Avery scoffs. I blink at her, one eyebrow lifted.

"She was with him on that voyage," she says. "She was with him on *every* voyage. They ran the fleet together."

Now both my eyebrows go up. That's not at all what our script says. Maria is almost a side character, motivation only for my Captain Small, whose arch of resilience is the drive that mirrors Havensboro's own hardiness.

Even five years ago, I wouldn't have thought twice about a story focusing on a man's journey and letting the woman serve as a background thought.

Now, though, I immediately see all the holes in the script.

And I feel like an absolute moron for not seeing it sooner.

"Oh, shit," I say to Maria's display box. "This complicates things."

Avery chuckles. "Complicates the truth? Hollywood does seem to have a problem with that." She pauses. "I'm guessing the script didn't account much for Maria?"

"Unfortunately, no."

"So…is that why you're here? To change it?"

I smile at her. "Yes." My face falls and I catch myself tapping on my thigh. "It'll ruffle some feathers, though."

I'm already imagining the call I'll make to the director and producer. They won't be pleased with a rewrite this late into the process, but I'm not going to tell a half-assed story.

Avery's shoulders lift higher, her body kind of caving in on itself. "Oh. I'm sorry."

"Why?"

"For…spoiling the truth, I guess. I don't know. You just got kind of severe."

My lips lift. I shift closer to her, and the part of me that'd been so focused on this research blissfully shuts the hell up.

The low lighting takes on a sultry twist, bathing Avery in shadows and divots that highlight her curves. I'm suddenly viscerally aware of how alone we are, the ever-present shushing of the ocean waves through the far window the only noise outside of our breaths.

Avery's chest rises, her breasts pulling taut against the overalls and tank top. My eyes hook there, watching the swell, the fall, and when she moans softly, I flick my gaze back up to her.

"I should thank you, actually," I say to her.

"For pointing out the problems with the movie?"

"Yes." I inch closer, and she starts to match me backwards until her spine hits the wall.

I stop. Did I misread this? But the look on her face is aching, a mirror of my own agonizing arousal—her cheeks are flushed, her eyes half-lidded, her lips parted in quick, sharp breaths.

"Avery," I purr her name. My cock twitches. "Let me thank you properly. Can I?"

CHAPTER FOUR: AVERY

Yes.

Oh *god*, yes.

I nod, my body pinned to the wall. It's only because I've absolutely never in my life done anything even remotely voyeuristic that I backed away from him. At any moment, Clarice could barge in on us. At any moment, literally anyone on Havensboro could find us. Unlikely, considering the nature of the museum; but still.

It's way more exciting than I ever thought something like this would be.

I nod again, desperation churning through me. "Yes."

Tom's eyes take on a feral twist. He plants his hands on either side of my body against the wall and I get a burst of his spicy cologne again.

His face angles down to mine and he exhales over my lips, making me unconsciously bend up towards him, not yet touching, just drawn in, a magnet. His breath is warm as it ghosts over me, another delicate exhale, another excruciating invisible pull.

"I wanted to taste you the moment I saw you," he says into my mouth. His tongue darts out, flicks at my upper lip, and my head knocks back against the wall.

"Then do it," I tell him. It comes out angry; I'm wound up, on the edge already, and he's *torturing* me.

He chuckles. "Oh, but I savor delicacies such as this," he says, and my *god*, that accent deepens, an English whirr that has me fisting my hands in his shirt. My knuckles brush his abs, unsurprisingly rock hard and rippling. They're begging to be touched—I dive my hands up under his shirt, playing in the lines between his muscles.

Slowly, so fucking slowly, he brushes his lips across mine. His tongue shoots out in quick, short licks that taste my top lip, my bottom; he clamps his mouth to mine and sucks my tongue into his mouth, tangling the two together.

My body arches up against him and he wraps one hand around my waist, holding me flush to him. His hard cock pins between our bodies and makes my pussy ache.

"Your moans taste so good, darling," he tells me and starts a trail of kisses down the side of my neck, nipping and licking his way to my collarbone. The straps of my tank top and bra slide down my arm and he hooks his finger in it, tugging it harder, pulling and pulling until my breast pops out.

I whimper, but only with need—I want him to see me. I'm nowhere near as ripped as he is, but I've got a body I'm quite proud of. I want to strip the rest of my clothes off and watch him look at all of me, because the way he's looking at my breast now, like it's the most entrancing thing he's ever seen, has me undone.

A brutal growl bubbles in his throat. "So fucking sweet," he murmurs into my skin, and then his mouth is on my breast, delivering the same tender, torturous licks he gave to my mouth. His hot breath coasts over the dimpled flesh and he flicks his tongue out, just grazing the tip of my nipple, indeed savoring it.

I writhe, but he holds me firm.

"Tom—*please*."

"Please what, darling?"

"Please—keep going—"

He smiles, and latches that smile onto my breast, taking my full nipple into his mouth. His tongue swirls around the tip, pulling it; and then he bites down, lightly, and I cry out.

"Shh," he laughs, coming back up to kiss away my outburst, "can't have Ms. McDermott hating me more than she does."

"No, of course not," I gasp. "That's what's important, after all."

"Indeed." He's grinning wickedly.

He hovers his lips on top of mine. His fingers are working at the other strap of my overalls. A click, a slither, and it falls off.

"I want to taste of all you," he tells me, and my knees weaken. "You deserve a proper thank you, after all."

Yes, yes, I do. I don't even know what I'm really agreeing to, just that I need more of him, more of *this*. Each touch sets fire to the chemistry we'd had in the diner, electricity ramped all the way up, explosion imminent. Every spark of his touch on my skin sizzles through me; his eyes on my body makes me feel impossibly sexy, some kind of goddess of sin and salvation come to life before him.

I want whatever he has to offer.

I want it all.

My overalls are already hanging on just to my hips. I push them the rest of the way down my body, letting them pool around my ankles. I'm left in just my pink tank top, one breast hanging out, and Tom sees now that I'm not wearing any panties.

His eyes bulge. He teeters, catching himself on the wall by my head. "Darling, what you do to me."

"The better question," I pant, "is what are you going to do to me?"

He growls. Lips curling up, eyes all pupil, absolutely vicious, and I feel a surge between my legs, wetness, ready for him.

He doesn't rip open his pants, though.

Tom drops to his knees, running his hands down my body, pulling the other strap of my tank top and bra down as he goes. My shirt and bra bunches around my waist and he fills each hand with a breast, kneading, rolling his palms over my nipples as he lowers his face to my pussy.

"Tom," I gasp his name, and he blows gently on the sensitive skin above my thighs.

His hands slip off my breasts to trickle down, grabbing one thigh, sliding it to the side. He has a full view of me; he can see my wetness, my eagerness for him.

"So wet," he says and slides a finger down my folds. He pushes it in and I whine, biting down the noise in my throat. "So wet for me."

He pulls his finger out, the tip glistening with moisture, and slides it into his mouth the same way I licked the whipped cream from my thumb. Indulgently, his eyes rolling shut, a low moan echoing in his throat.

He doesn't say anything else. He leans in and strokes long licks through my folds like each taste makes him hungry for more. I can hear him moaning with pleasure as much I hear my own moans, our pleasure mingling as we fight and fail to keep it quiet.

My body bucks against the wall with each expert lick he gives me, that vicious tongue sliding up, swirling around my clit, diving back down. He traces every inch of me, leaving nothing untouched until I'm vibrating with building need.

"Tom—I'm so close, please—"

He moans his assent. Those lips land on my clit, kissing deeply, before he sucks in, pulling my clit into his mouth.

I scream into my lips, keening like a madwoman. The orgasm tears at every nerve in fireworks that will incinerate me inside out, but I don't care, let it burn me, let me fall apart here and now. He keeps sucking through my climax, dragging every ounce of pleasure from my twitching clit, until my stifled screams turn to whimpers.

He hauls himself back up my body, kissing each nipple, my neck, my cheeks. He curls his arms around me and I go limp against him, sweat sheening my skin, my breaths coming in gasping breaths.

"Avery," he says my name into my mouth, and I kiss him, tasting myself on him. And fuck, that just ignites me even more—I need this man inside of me, need him more fiercely than I've ever felt—

"You have a room here?" I gasp.

He grins against me. I feel his lips lift. "Yes. 211."

"Go. Let's go." I scramble out of his arms and roughly tug on my overalls, tucking myself back into my bra and tank top.

He chuckles but catches my wrist as I dart past him for the door. I swing on him and he grabs the back of my neck, cradling my head in the museum's low light.

The pause reorients me, helps me see through my fog of desire.

There's something on his face now, a pinch to his brows, a gravity in his eyes.

"Avery," he says my name again. God, I don't think I'll ever get tired of the way he says it. "There is nothing I would like more than to throw you on my bed and continue showing that body just how quickly I am becoming obsessed with you, but I have to tell you something first."

I go still. "Oh god, you're married?"

He smiles. "No. Far from it. Perpetually single, the tabloids say."

Tabloids?

Why would tabloids care about a movie producer?

My mind trips.

He *is* a producer. Isn't he?

I stare at him, this time, analytically.

Those green eyes. That chiseled jaw. That smile that I've seen on magazine covers and late night interviews and in a dozen movies—

My eyes fly all the way open.

Oh my god.

I'd thought I'd recognized him. But why the *fuck* would *he* be on this island early, and alone, and so unabashedly flirting with a small-town waitress? No. No *way*.

"I'm Tom Hudel," he tells me. His smile is kind of sad, but I refuse to let it get to me. "As in…"

"*Tom Hudel*," I repeat.

I back away from him. My mind is blank, so I'm not entirely sure *why* I'm backing away from him, just that I need to not be touching him right now.

I can't think with his hands on me.

His mouth on my skin. Sucking on my clit. His—

See? Exactly. *Fuck* I can't *think.*

"Avery." He pins his hands to his sides like he's fighting trying to reach for me. "I should have told you who I was once I'd realized you hadn't recognized me. But I—"

"Yeah, you should have." Anger surges up my chest, heats my skin. "So this was part of your Havensboro research?"

"*No,*" he says with such force that I almost believe him. "I didn't plan on meeting you. I didn't plan on—please, Avery. Let me explain."

But I'm already backing towards the door, tugging my overall straps into place, shaking my head.

No. No. *Fuck* no.

I need air. I need air right now.

I turn and kick through the door, racing back through the inn. Clarice is at her desk now and she gives me a disapproving frown as I grab my coat and fly out into the drizzle that is now full-on rain.

How could I have been such an idiot? I knew he was connected to the movie, but *fuck*, why didn't I recognize him? Maybe I just didn't *want* to recognize him. But Gwen didn't know who he was, either; what the *fuck*.

Does it matter who he is? Does it really change anything? I'd gone in knowing this would be a one-time thing. I'm leaving; he's leaving. Does him being *Tom fucking Hudel* really change any of this, except to make it slightly more exciting, because he's a literal goddamn dreamboat?

I jog across the street for the diner. By the time I get there, I'm soaked through and shivering and absolutely torn in half.

I need perspective. Desperately.

Gwen is still behind the counter. She sees me and her eyes form perfect saucers.

"Danny, I'm taking my twenty," she shouts to the cook in the back. He protests, but she and I both are rushing down the diner on either side of the bar.

We hit the end and shove into the employee's only room.

"What happened?" Gwen grabs a towel from a stack near the dryer and starts sopping the water out of my hair. "Did he…try something?"

"No, no. I mean, yes? But only—fuck, Gwen. *Fuck*."

"Okay, sit." She pushes me into a chair and takes one across from me. "Talk. Now. Sentences, not cusswords."

"He ate me out in the Havensboro Museum."

"I'm sorry, *what*?"

"Yeah. Right? *Right?* What the fuck—"

"Avery. Focus."

I let my face fall into my hands. I can still smell his cologne on my palms, spicy and hot. My pussy aches anew. Clearly *that* part of me has forgiven him.

"He's Tom Hudel," I moan into my hands.

Gwen chirps. "Tom…Hudel."

"Yeah."

"*Tom Hudel,* Tom Hudel? As in the *actor*? As in the guy who was in that superhero—"

"Yep."

"And was in that movie with the actress who—"

"That one too."

"And was *naked* in that French flick—"

"Oh my god, I forgot about that one."

"That's why he looked so familiar! Though I'd have recognized him sooner without his clothes on."

I flip my face up to Gwen. "Oh my *god*, he really is huge, isn't he? Oh my *fuck*—"

"Avery, sentences!"

"Tom Hudel ate me out in the Havensboro Museum."

"Yeah, I got that. So—" Gwen's eyes go wild, like she's losing her grip on reality. "Why in the ever-living fuck are you over here with me?"

Because...he didn't tell me?

He didn't tell me until *after* he gave me the best orgasm of my life.

But he did tell me *before* he got his own release, which for a guy is pretty massive.

So...

"I—" Sentences, sentences, do not cuss. "I have absolutely no idea."

Gwen shrieks, and she sounds like she's dying. She looks like it, too; eyes rolled back, fingers clawing at her face. "Oh my god, I will *kill* you, Avery Watson. Death, death a hundred times over, if you do not get your hot little ass back to that museum and fuck his living brains out. Tell me you did not run out on him *naked*?"

"No, he was clothed. I, um, wasn't."

"Avery." Gwen sobers and points at me. "I tell you this as your very married friend. You go fuck that super-hot celebrity and *then* come back here and tell me all about it. Do you understand me?"

"He'll leave, though." The words surprise even me.

I *know* he'll leave. That was never in question.

Why does it make my chest hurt?

"*So?*" Gwen screeches. "You're leaving too."

"I know."

"So what's the problem?"

"I—nothing." I stand. Because nothing *is* the problem. I can do this, have a fling with a celebrity, and then part ways amicably, without drama.

I've never been a one-night stand kind of girl, though.

And already, all I can think about— aside from Tom's sexy body—is the passion in his eyes when we talked about Havensboro history and his movie. He lit up with a kind of devotion I had never seen before, the exact kind of passion I'm leaving Havensboro to find.

But he came to me, it turns out.

And then he'll leave.

No. I won't think about that. I just *won't*. This will quite possibly be the best sex of my life, and I won't miss out on it just because my heart is getting attached.

I nod. Nod again. And I turn to the door.

"Go get him, girl," Gwen says and smacks my ass.

I give her a two fingered salute. But I'm shaking.

I slip out of the employee room and get halfway to the door when something catches my eye.

Oh. Maybe *that's* why I came here. Huh.

I grab the object off the table and hurry back out into the rain.

CHAPTER FIVE: TOM

"You want them to rewrite *what*?"

I sigh into my phone. "Maria's role. Total overhaul. She needs to be as much a crux of the movie as the Captain."

"Tom. Have you lost your mind? Filming starts in six days."

"I know. But a lot of the early scenes won't change, she's in those. We just build on those scenes. It'll solidify the whole project. Just—set up a meeting with the producers and director, will you? I'll convince them."

"No, no, I'll handle this." My manager sighs heavily. I'd be lying if I said I hadn't heard that sigh a hundred times before. "Just get into your right headspace. This hasn't thrown you for a loop too much, has it?"

"No."

"Are you sure? How'd you even find out about Maria, anyway?"

My mouth goes dry. "A, um, local helped me."

"Ah, they're not icing you out?"

I look around my hotel room. My very empty hotel room. "Nope. Not icing me out at all."

"Good. Good. That bodes well for the crew. All right, I'll be in touch once I get yelled at by the producers."

"Thanks, Mark. You're the best."

"Yeah, yeah." He hangs up.

I drop my phone onto the desk and stand there a beat, staring at the dark screen. I was dumb enough not to get Avery's number. I know where she works, though. How desperate would it make me to show up at the diner tonight? Maybe tomorrow?

Shit. I pinch the skin between my eyes. I knew I should've told Avery who I was right from the start.

But we'd had a connection. I know she'd felt it too. It *wasn't* just about sex— though, fuck, I'd give up sugar if it meant tasting her pussy again. I'd never felt anything as blissful as having her clit in my mouth while she came, seeing her eyes roll back, her sweet body arching and glistening in the museum's lights.

My cock stiffens and I thump my fist on the desk. Goddammit. How do I make this up to her? How do I prove that I'm not just into her for the sex? I know the movie wraps in a few weeks, but we can make those few weeks heaven. And after? I don't know. I don't know, but I do know that I want to try.

She makes me want to try.

There's a knock on my door.

I groan and pad across the room. Did Ms. McDermott find out I tongue-fucked Avery in her museum? Oh shit—were there security cameras? That's what I need, a tabloid explosion of a sex scandal—

I open the door.

And my mind grinds to a halt.

Avery stands there, dripping wet. She parts her lips and I can't believe my luck.

"Tom," she starts. "I wanted to…apologize."

I huff. "You owe me nothing, Avery. I'm the one who's sorry. I shouldn't have waited to tell you the truth."

"I shouldn't have freaked out like that. I just…" Her voice trails off. She has her arms behind her back, making her raincoat pop open, showing spots of raindrops on her pink tank top. "I don't usually do this."

"Do what?"

Avery takes a deep breath. Her eyes stay on mine, and there's a hunger in her suddenly, one that stokes need into my now fully hard cock.

She pulls her hand out from behind her back and shows me what she's holding.

A cannister of whipped cream.

My eyes bulge.

Oh. *Oh.*

I grab her wrist and drag her inside. Once the door is safely shut and locked, Avery giggles, and fuck if that doesn't make my dick heave with longing.

She sets the cannister on the desk and pulls out of her raincoat, letting it drop to the ground behind her. Every movement is slow, sure, and any tentativeness is gone from her.

But…

I cradle her face in my hands. "I don't usually do this, either."

Her eyebrow goes up. "Oh?"

"No. So you should know—" I kiss one eyelid. "—that I don't plan on being done with you—" the other, and she gasps, "—for a very long time."

"I think I could be okay with that," she whispers, her voice hoarse.

Her overalls drop to the ground. She was unbuttoning them while I kissed her, the clever girl. And when she hefts her tank top over her head, standing before me fully naked, I have to bite down on my tongue, hard, not to blow my load right there.

"Lay down on the bed," I order. I don't know where it comes from—I'm only this demanding on set, when the integrity of the film depends on it. But it creeps up from the core of me, and Avery's eyes darken with lust.

She obeys, sprawling herself on the comforter, her wet hair fanned across the pillows.

I grab the whipped cream.

"It's not fair," she says and juts her chin at my chest. "You're still fully clothed."

I glance down, back to her. "Well, if you're a good girl and don't make a sound, maybe I'll take off my clothes, hm?"

"Don't make a sound?" Her eyebrows twist.

I bend over and flutter my lips across her forehead. "Someday, I'll take you some place where you can scream your pleasure to the ceiling—but for now, I need you biting that gorgeous lip and staying quiet, darling."

"But you already—" She blushes.

"I already got you off?" I lick the corner of her mouth. "Why would one be enough? You left, after all. I think you need to make it up to me."

Avery's breath catches. I can smell the desire coming off her, liquid heat that makes her legs tremble.

I shake the whipped cream canister and angle the nozzle over her nipple, brushing the ridges gently back and forth over her tips, eliciting a soft groan from her. She immediately bites down on her lip and closes her eyes.

"Ah-ah, eyes open, darling," I tell her. "I want you watching what I do to you."

"*Fuck,* Tom—"

I squirt a dollop of the frigid whipped cream on one nipple. Avery hisses, arching, eyes rolling back. I repeat the process on her other nipple, then I reach down, part her lips, and leave a sizable swirl on her clit.

She's writhing by now. The cold sensation of the cream has to be driving her mad.

I toss the cannister onto the desk chair but take a second to admire my work. Avery has her hands fisted in the bedspread, her chest heaving, making her whipped cream nipple coverings tremble. Her legs are spread, showing me her glistening pussy lips, the cream starting to melt down to her ass.

Avery's fluttering eyes find mine, and I can see the pleasure building in her, a dam straining, aching.

My dick aches too, balls clenching, desperate to release inside her. But I'm equally desperate to taste her again and feel her come apart on my tongue, and if I get a little sugar with the sugar? This is *heaven*.

I crawl up the bed, hovering just above Avery, and attack one nipple, sucking the whipped cream into my mouth. She mewls into her closed lips and I continue my torment on the other nipple, licking and sucking, reveling in the taste and feel of her in my mouth.

I make sure her nipples both thoroughly cleaned by rolling them through my fingers in a way that has her throwing her head back into the blankets.

I chuckle, and she gives me a look that's all heat, lost in her building desire.

"Taste me, Tom," she begs, and fuck, it's the sweetest thing I've ever heard, the sheer *need* in her voice. "Please."

"How can I say no to such a request?" I crawl down to put my knees on the floor, then I drag her ass back towards me, on the edge of the bed. She's spread wide and dripping in her own juices and the whipped cream—it's a feast.

I start at that birthmark on her thigh, the one I'd wanted to taste the moment I saw it in the diner. It was too dark in the museum to see it, but there it is, tempting and teasing me exactly where the line of her shorts would be.

Her thigh ripples a little when I lick it, a shiver of pleasure.

I move to her ass and lick all the way up, gathering as much of the whipped cream as I can into my mouth. Her body jolts but she doesn't make a sound, and when I peek up at her, she has her eyes closed again, her lips pinched in a tight line, every muscle in her face clenched.

My dick is uncomfortably hard against my jeans, but I'm not done yet, not by a long shot.

I shove my tongue deep into her pussy, satisfied by the soft gasp she lets herself have.

Then I replace my tongue with two fingers—no, three—and begin pumping steadily. She's so fucking tight, her muscles rippling around my fingers, and I can only imagine what it'll feel like to have my cock wedged inside her, at the mercy of her pulsing need. But first, she'll come again, she'll come so hard that all memory of her walking out on me will be wiped from her mind.

She damn near exploded when I did this last time, so I suction my lips around her clit, and I suck slowly, slowly, taking each part of it into my mouth in small increments.

"Tom," she whines. "Oh, fuck, *Tom*."

I release the suction. My fingers keep pumping, and I arch them forward, finding that spot just behind her clit. "Yeah, baby?"

"Keep doing that, please—"

"Doing what?"

"Su-sucking, sucking there, please."

"You like your clit in my mouth, darling?"

"Yes, fuck, *yes*."

"Such language." I grin and push that grin against her clit, letting her feel my teeth on that sensitive bud. She cries out but quickly stifles it in her arm as I keep up my assault with my fingers, pushing her closer and closer to the edge.

Then I give her what she wants. I lock my lips back around her clit and suck the full of it into my mouth, flicking it all over with the sharp edge of my tongue. Avery comes with a muffled scream, her pussy walls clenching so hard around my fingers that my dick practically pops in jealousy.

As she comes down from her high, I lick up her juices, cleaning the last of the whipped cream from her crevices. She falls back on the bed, arms splayed, hair wild, and when she sees me watching, she props up onto her elbows.

"Was I quiet enough?" she asks drowsily, and the innocent way she tips her head has me downright *feral*.

"Oh yes, darling," I tell her and push up to kiss her. Our lips meet in a crash of need, but I feel her fingers tugging at my shirt, my pants.

"If you insist," I say, and I yank my shirt over my head.

CHAPTER SIX: AVERY

Most of the world has seen Tom Hudel's body before. The photos of his nude role in that one French movie are all over the internet, but my *god*, nothing could have prepared me for seeing him in the flesh.

He's a masterpiece. The muscles that had been painstakingly sculpted even under his long sleeve shirt are just the tip of it; everything on his body is lean, flexed, and solid. Not bulky, but strong all the same.

And his cock.

Oh, my.

It's as long as the rest of him, fully erect and bulging purple with veins. It looks almost painful, the head glossed with pre-cum, and I reach out, wrapping my fingers around the long shaft, wanting to relieve his ache.

"Oh *fuck*," I curse, realization dawning on me. "Condoms! Shit, shit—"

"That mouth, Avery, tsk tsk." Tom kisses me quiet. "Don't worry. Even though I rarely use them, my agent always stocks some in my luggage. Occupational hazard."

I pause for a second, trying to decide if I should be worried by that, but then I just throw my head back and laugh. Tom leaves for half a second and returns, rolling a condom over his length.

I pout. "I could've done that."

He kisses me again, and I feel his smile. "Next time, darling."

He says *next time* with a growl that goes straight to my still-throbbing clit, my whole pussy warm and pulsing with the receding ebbs of orgasm, but still ready and open for him.

I lay back, arms over my head. Tom whimpers at the sight of my breasts stretching between us and tucks his arm underneath me to brace himself as he sucks my nipple into his mouth.

Then he thrusts inside me in one easy push, and I cry out, all ecstasy at the delicious feel of him sheathed to the hilt.

"Shh, darling," he says, laughter in his voice.

"That might not happen," I moan and shift under him. "You feel too good."

My movement has his eyes rolling shut. I do it again and he props up, one hand on either side of my head, and gives a hard lurch against my hips.

I mewl, remembering to bite my lips together, but *fuck*.

"Oh, darling, *you* are the one who feels too good." He thrusts again, the muscles in his neck contracting, and he manages to open his eyes enough to look down at me. His pupils are huge, dark with desire, and he thrusts again, building a steady pace that shoots tingles through every nerve ending in my body. "I'm not going to last with a pussy as tight as this. Do you have any idea how good you feel around my cock? You make me want to wax poetic, Avery."

He's thrusting still, hammering into my pussy walls in a way that *does* feel poetic. It ignites my body, makes my clit ache, my nipples tightening, and all the while I keep my lips tightly shut, too afraid to open them at all. The moment I do, I'll scream, because I've never in my life had someone who just inherently knows what to do to make my body respond.

Like the way Tom tucks his arms around my waist and rocks his hips down and forward, finding my G-spot with effortless ease. I whimper, but he's holding me tight to him; nowhere to go, nowhere to escape the overwhelming pleasure as he drives his long cock deep, deep into my pussy, hitting my G-spot, his pelvis rubbing my clit over, and over, and—

I scream, and Tom swallows it with his mouth. I fall apart when I hear him moaning right back at me, his control fraying as he comes in tandem with me. I knot my arms around his neck, riding him as much as he rides me, the two of us tangled in pleasure and soft, brittle moans.

We come down, and he falls to the bedspread next to me and disposes of the condom in the garbage bin by the bedside table. He's back instantly, before I even have a chance to worry what to do next; Tom pulls me up against him, the two of us deliciously naked still, our limbs entwining.

My heart is still going a million miles a minute. I lay with my head on his chest, one leg strewn over his, the thoughts in my head flying.

Holy shit.

Holy *shit*.

Tom trails his fingers up my arm, sending goosebumps flaring out. "What are you thinking, darling?"

I tuck my chin to his chest to contain my manic grin. "That I adore when you call me *darling*. Or," and here I can't stop the bolt of unease that zips like lightning through my belly, "is that so you don't mess up my name?"

In a flash, Tom has me flipped onto my back, my arms pinned against the pillows. His green eyes are insistent, severe in a way that stuns me silent.

"Avery," he tells me. "Avery—" His eyes go wide, horror.

"Watson," I fill in for him, which is forgivable since I never even told him my last name.

"Watson," he repeats, and he smiles, his face full of reverence. His cheeks are pink now in the most adorable way. "Avery Watson. Would you like to know the last time I slept with anyone?"

"Well. I—"

"Two years ago."

I stare at him. "I'm sorry, it sounded like you said two *years*."

"That's right." Tom sits up, pulling me with him, and my hair falls in long tangles around my face that he brushes behind my ears. "I am not one for flippant relationships, Avery. And usually when I court a woman—"

"Court?" Oh god, I'm melting, I'm a puddle on the floor.

"—I spend at least a few weeks beforehand wooing her." He kisses my cheekbone. "Sending her flowers." My nose. "Taking her on ridiculously expensive dates at insanely high-end restaurants." My other cheekbone. "And just generally lavishing her in my affection. Then, and only then, do I hope she will allow me the honor of making her mine."

"So what changed?" My voice is raspy. My nipples are piqued again, my whole body alive with sensation.

Tom pulls back to look into my eyes. "You, Avery. I knew the moment I saw you that you would be important. And the fact that we have so quickly come to the point of devouring one another means I will merely have to work extra hard to make sure you feel, in every way, cherished."

I kiss him, cupping his sharp jaw in my palm, savoring the tenderness in his lips, his gentle, lapping tongue. I could so easily fall for this man—

My mind stumbles to a halt.

He's leaving when the movie is done.

I'm leaving, probably sooner, if the money he gave me at the diner is as much as I think it was. I've been planning this escape from Havensboro for most of my life—a chance to break out into something that's truly *mine*. To be free and wild and taste the world.

I wrap my arms around Tom's neck and pull him down on top of me, arching my body up against his.

Can I give up my dreams for this man? Would *he* give up his dreams for me?

His words are so beautiful that they make me want to shuck all my plans and follow him around like a panting puppy. But that's exactly it—I'm not, and I refuse to be.

Tom pulls back, hovering over me. "Tell me what you're thinking, Avery."

He says it softly, but I can see the worry dimpling his eyebrows. Can he read me that well already?

"I'm thinking that this is too good to be true," I admit, hating that I break this moment between us. "And around here, if something feels too good to be true, it *always* is."

He cocks his head. "That's fair, but—it feels like there's something else. I'm afraid you know far more about me than I know about you, darling. Tell me what you're really thinking. Please."

I put my thumb on his bottom lip. Fuck, I love him begging.

"I'm leaving Havensboro," I tell him.

He frowns. "When?"

"Soon." I could leave tomorrow once I count the money and know it's enough.

Tom kisses my thumb, my palm. "My movie starts filming in a week. Give me that time, Avery Watson. Give me that time to prove to you that this is real."

"By buying me flowers and taking me to fancy dinners…at the diner where I work, because it's the only restaurant on the island?"

Tom grins. "By opening my heart to you and encouraging you to open your heart to me. One week. Please."

I sigh. *Oh, my heart is already wide open, and that's what I'm afraid of.*

Because, by the end of the week, I have to leave Havensboro no matter what. I don't want to be the kind of girl who gives up all her plans for a guy.

For a guy who also happens to be a celebrity, and while I certainly don't blame him for his baggage, I'm still downright terrified of the life he's asking of me.

But I kiss him again. "All right. One week."

CHAPTER SEVEN: TOM

It damn near breaks my heart to let Avery leave my hotel room even for a moment, but she needs to change and shower—though I begged her to join me in mine. She promised to return with enough clothes and toiletries to last at least a few nights with me here.

While she's gone, I plan.

Part of what makes me so attuned to acting is how thoroughly I commit myself to things I'm passionate about. I fall into each role wholly, fully, heart and soul.

Which is how I feel about Avery.

She has me, heart and soul, and now I have to prove it.

She wants to leave Havensboro—which is all the better, honestly. I want to sweep her away, show her the world. But she has her own plans. So how do I convince her that I don't want her to give up her dreams—I want her to braid her dreams with mine?

I shower quickly, restyling myself in fresh black jeans and a button-up, and by the time Avery knocks on my door again, I've already set my plan into motion with a few strategic phone calls.

I open the door. She's changed into a sweater over jeans and a tight t-shirt, simple and comfortable and altogether tantalizing. I sweep her into my arms. God, she fits against my body so well, the perfect, delicate bend of her stomach against the plane of mine, her breasts tucking up under my chest.

She's the one who kisses me first, and it makes me moan into her lips.

"Is that how we're going to spend the week?" Avery giggles against me. "No complaints, honestly."

"It will be a large part of this week, to be sure." I take her bag and toss it onto the desk, then I grab my hotel key and phone. "But I have far more devious plans in mind."

"Oh?" A bolt of worry crosses her face.

I kiss her cheek and take her hand. "How about some lunch, darling?"

We go back outside. The rain has alleviated now, leaving a blue sky stretching wide over the island. I'm hit again with the same sense of fate that came when I first landed this morning. This place is truly magical.

I can easily see why Havensboro was such a source of motivation for my character in *Run Aground*. That, and his Maria.

I tuck Avery up alongside me, my arm around her waist, desperate to keep her close as I lead her across the road.

"When do you work next?" I ask her.

"Tomorrow night."

"Ah." I can't keep the disappointment out of my voice. One night less to woo her.

Avery bats her eyelashes up at me. Fuck, but it's sexy. "Surely a few hours away from each other won't upset your master plan?"

I press my lips to her ear. "But a few more hours without my cock buried inside you? That will surely be upsetting to us both."

Avery sways closer to me, capturing my lips, and I all but throw her against the side of the diner and fuck her senseless right there.

With great restraint, I open the diner's door and guide her inside.

The lunch crowd seems to be in full swing, but a corner booth is designated for us. In it, already sipping icy cups of water, are Avery's friend Gwen and her husband.

That was the first call I'd made: to Gwen at the diner.

Avery gives me a curious look, but she's smiling. "What is this?"

"A double date." I grin at her. "I want to know everything about you, and you seemed close to your fellow waitress, so I thought—" Sudden panic has my eyes wide. "Did I misread your relationship? Is she not your friend beyond work?"

Avery puts her hand on the center of my chest as we cross the diner, still entwined in each other. I feel heads turning, staring; is it because they recognize me, or because Avery has a new man, or both?

"She's my best friend," Avery says, and I exhale. "But her husband is my ex-boyfriend."

An empty laugh echoes out of me. "What?"

Avery shrugs. "Small island. The single scene rotates through itself rather…efficiently."

I come to a stop a few feet from the corner booth, sure my amused horror is clear on my face. "How…how big is the single scene on Havensboro?"

She comes up onto her toes and kisses the shell of my ear. "Jealous, Hudel?"

I growl and grab her ass. "Of everyone who has gotten to spend more time with you than I have. I pity every person who had their hands on you and didn't realize what a succulent treasure you are."

She's trembling against me. The heat in her eyes intensifies, and she wraps her fist in the front of my shirt.

Why did I insist we leave my hotel room? Why am I not cock deep inside of her right this moment?

"Avery!" her friend Gwen says from the booth. "We're over here!"

She's giggling as she calls to us. And when I break away, I see we have the attention of most of the diner, including no small number of young families with gawking children.

Shame flares pink to my cheeks. So quickly I'm forgoing my usual caution around public displays. I subtly rearrange my hard cock and lead Avery to the corner booth.

She squeezes my hand and gives me a private, laughing smile, and a shrug as if to say *Small town, what can you do?*

Avery and I slide into the booth across from Gwen and, apparently, Avery's ex. The man has his arm around his wife, and he takes a sip of his water, his lips clearly fighting a smile.

"So, Avery." Gwen perches her elbows on the table. "Are you going to officially introduce us?"

Avery puts her hand on my thigh under the table. I drape my arm along the back of the booth, arranging myself against her, and again I think of how well she fits my body.

"This is Tom," Avery says, squeezing my thigh. "Tom, this is Gwen and Kevin."

Kevin gives a nod. Gwen beams at me, her whole face red, like she's trying hard not to spew a million questions at us.

She'll get her chance—I have questions to ask, too.

I stroke my fingers idly up and down Avery's shoulder as a waitress sets out water glasses for Avery and me. We order, and then I bend forward, matching Gwen.

We spend the next hour, Gwen and I, punting questions back and forth in what has to be the most animated game of twenty questions I've ever been part of—including the stints I've done on late night shows. For every question I have, Gwen fires one right back, and no topic seems off limits. I feel Avery tensing next to me at questions like *What are your intentions for Avery?* and *What was the name of that model you banged again?* The last question Gwen asks in between bites of a key lime pie dessert, thrown out casually, trying to trip me up.

"I don't *bang* anyone," I tell her with a smile. "You can Google for proof if you'd like."

Gwen does just that, and then she asks me detailed questions about every sordid story she finds on the internet.

I don't mind. For every question she asks, I get an answer from her about Avery.

I learn that she's known Avery since childhood. That Avery has indeed been talking about leaving Havensboro for just as long—not for any particular career, but merely just to get *away*, to have something of her own. Avery blushes as Gwen goes on about younger Avery's dedication to escaping, and I can tell more and more that this is important to her. Independence.

It makes my chest ache. But my own job comes with required independence, long stints in remote filming locations with little time to travel. So if—when—we make this work, there will be plenty of opportunity for Avery to keep her dream lifestyle, wherever that may be.

By the time lunch is over, I know as much about Avery as I'd hoped to learn. Her favorite color, food, movie. That she's an only child. That she was only with Kevin for about two weeks before they broke up, and Kevin clearly holds no lingering feelings towards Avery; he was utterly entranced by his wife most of the meal, tucking her hair behind her ear, rubbing her back. My actions with Avery mirrored them, always touching her in some way, reminding her that though I was talking mostly with Gwen, she was the real reason we were here.

I could have gotten much of this information from Avery herself, but the look on her face as we leave the diner is confirmation that I did the right thing.

"Gwen *loves* you," she coos at me. Her phone buzzes and she pulls it out of her pocket. "Yep. She just texted—she's leaving Kevin and going to try to break us up."

I twirl her, right there in the deserted street, and pull her flush with my chest, our hands arranged in a dancing position. We start to sway slowly, and Avery blushes a beautiful shade of red.

"Unfortunately, I'm besotted by her best friend," I tell her. "And I think Kevin is far too in love to let Gwen go, either."

"Yeah, it was clear to everyone that they were the better pair immediately," Avery says. She leans into me, her eyes darting around us. "People are watching."

"I don't care," I say, and surprisingly, I mean it. The lack of paparazzi is utterly freeing. A few phones might flash with photos that will find their way online, but let the world know—Avery is mine, and I am hers.

"So." Avery pushes up to kiss me. "What next, Casanova? Dinner with my parents?"

"Oh, my darling. You're all mine now."

CHAPTER EIGHT: AVERY

"Are you sure about this?"

I balance on the bobbing starboard deck, one eyebrow cocked. "You don't trust me, Hudel?"

Tom tips his head. "With my life, darling. But I reserved a captain to sail this vessel as well."

This vessel. I feel my cheeks heating. How dare he be so cute?

The sequel to our lunch date with Gwen is a sailing venture around Havensboro. And while I did like the idea of letting someone else steer the small boat Tom rented, I like even more the idea of being alone with him, out on the open water.

"Every kid on Havensboro grows up learning to sail. It's in our blood." I kick off, pushing the boat out into the water, away from the dock. "Don't worry. I won't let you drown. Besides, this is great firsthand experience for Captain Small, huh?"

Tom tips his head back, letting the salty sea breeze pick through his hair. The storm has passed, and the sun is high now, warm and golden on our skin. He's already shirked his wool coat, letting his long, lean arms stretch in the sun. I'm glad for my jeans and t-shirt, knowing how sweaty sailing usually makes me, but I suddenly wish I'd worn some flirty sundress that could catch a breeze and blow up, revealing all the parts of me that Tom has marked as his own already.

I spend a few minutes explaining the basics of sailing to Tom, which is easy enough with the motored boat. Soon, we're clipping along nicely.

Tom stands just behind me as I steer, his hands on my hips, and when I look up at him, his focus is on the shore, the skyline. I can't see his eyes behind his sunglasses, but he's smiling, a look of pure euphoria on his lips.

"There's a cove up here I want to show you," I call to him over the whipping wind. "Captain Small and Maria rode out the worst of the storm there before they could make it to the main dock."

Tom bends close, his lips to my ear. "Wonderful," he purrs against me, and then he takes my earlobe between his teeth and gently bites down. A shiver pulsates down to my toes and it's all I can do to keep steering the boat, pulling us into the relative shelter of the cove.

I cut the engine, drop the anchor, and spin my body to his. The boat rocks beneath us, gentle, lapping waves.

Tom's looking up at the walls of the cove, the jagged stone encompassing us on one side, the open ocean on the other.

"Now, a bit of Havensboro history," I say to him, pulling his eyes back to me. I glide his sunglasses up and perch them on his head. "Do you know how Captain Small and Maria survived that fated night here?"

Tom smirks. "I haven't the faintest idea, darling. How did they survive?"

"Well." I push my lips to his cheek, his jaw, trailing kisses down the side of his neck. "Rumors say they had to huddle together for warmth, and that nine months later, their first daughter was born."

"Ah. Clever sailors, were they?"

"And do you want to know what locals call this cove?" I hook my fingers in his belt and yank him closer to me, our bodies flush together, and he cranes his neck down to nip at my mouth.

"Hm." Is he all he says, because then I'm working free his belt, unzipping his pants.

"Swell Cove," I say, and I can't stop my grin. "Because of the ocean's swells, but also—"

I reach down and grab his cock. It's hard already and my pussy aches at just the touch. I need him in me, *now*.

But first...

I drop to my knees.

Tom's hands go to my hair, fingers dragging through the windblown strands. "Avery Watson, did you bring me to Havensboro's make-out spot?"

"Maybe." I smirk up at him, nose scrunched, all mischief.

"Naughty darling—" Tom hisses as I take him into my mouth.

He's gotten to taste me twice now, so it's only fair. I take my time sucking him deep into my throat, relaxing my muscles and feeling his girth fill every space. His hips buck against me, unconscious jerks that drive me wild, knowing I'm already getting him to the point of losing control.

I pull back and lick his shaft, root to tip, lapping up the drops of pre-cum before going back down and sucking his balls into my mouth, one by one.

His fingers dig into my hair. The only things coming out of his mouth are hisses and gulping moans. I'm lost in the little noises he makes, the way his eyes are closed and his face scrunched in concentration as I take him deep again. I plunge him all the way down, back up, down again, building a steady rhythm of fucking him with my mouth that has his body shuddering where I grip his hips.

"Avery, darling—" He gasps. "Stand. Stand now."

The desperation in his tone yanks me to my feet unbidden. I'm helpless not to follow his commands, and it should scare me—it might, were I not so frantically aroused by him too. I pull my shirt up and off, casting it aside; bra next. Tom rips my jeans down, and I'm not wearing panties again—I never might, with him.

There's a deeper pull between us, an energy of need that has Tom lifting me, my legs threading around his waist. I curl my arms around his shoulders and kiss him, tongue lashing with his, as he spins and lays me out on the long bench at the side of the boat. His shirt is off too, his tight abs and sculpted pecs gleaming with sea spray.

He pulls a condom out of his jean pocket before he kicks them to the side, and I make good on my promise—this time, I rip it open with my teeth and roll it down his length, taking a second to cup his balls in my palms, playing with them in my fingers.

Tom growls, a low, heavy reverberation that rushes straight to my clit. He shoves me back onto the bench and plows into me, no teasing, no words. Both of us are driven far enough, each moment we spend together a buildup in its own. Every touch, every look from him is foreplay.

His cock plunges deep into me, his thrusts manic, buoyed by the rise and fall of the boat in the ocean's currents. Each thrust pulls a cry from my lips and I revel in being able to make noise now.

Tom smiles at it, pressing kisses to the sides of my mouth. "That's right, darling. Tell me how good I make you feel."

His hand snakes between us to find my clit, and those long, expert fingers start working it in fast, relentless circles.

"Oh god, Tom—"

"Tell me how good you feel," he commands me, rubbing, *rubbing*. "Let me hear your pleasure. Come for me, darling."

Pleasure builds, and builds, and I come with a scream that rings off this hidden cove.

Tom is fast behind me, his body quaking with orgasm as he, too, shouts. My orgasm finds a second wave with his, ripping through my nerves in a frenzy of pleasure and pure, sweet, aching release.

We collapse together, our mouths finding each other, kisses just as desperate as our fucking. We're both sweaty and that only adds to it—I can't get enough of his mouth on me, and he feels the same, his eyebrows pinched like he's in pain.

The boat rocks, the peace of the ocean's gentle waves cocooning around us, so every kiss is enhanced, and I can almost believe this is a dream.

The next few days pass in a blur of lavish euphoria.

Tom definitely knows how to *woo* a woman. Every morning, I wake up to a tray of whatever fresh baked good he got up early to snag from Clarice's breakfast spread. We then spend the day flurrying around the island—he insists that I show him all of my favorite spots.

I take him to the beach where I would go swimming in high school.

We hit the ice cream shack near the north pier, and I about lose my mind with laughter when he takes on the dozen-scoop sundae challenge, and *wins* it, eating the whole thing in less than twenty minutes.

We even do a version of the polar dip and then immediately rush back to his hotel room, where he begs me to stay every night, and we warm up under the blankets, our bodies creating an incomparable heat.

The dates are amazing. The sex is even better. The moments when I have to break and go to work leave me in a foggy daze of happiness where all I can think about are his lips on my body, the look on his face when I tell him about growing up here, my likes and dislikes, everything. He's so attentive, soaking up information with a childlike enthusiasm; and he tells me just as much, going into animated detail about growing up in the UK, and how he came to the States to act, what it's like living in LA.

He skirts around his recent life, focusing only on the films he's done and the projects he has in the works, but I can tell, by the way he shrugs when I ask about his LA house, that he's lonely. It has to be a very solitary life, always jumping from one location to the next, with minimal stints in a house he rarely uses. It's probably why he works so much—to stay busy, as a distraction.

My heart aches, seeing the way he avoids the topic. The forced happiness. My heart aches over all of this, actually, every enchanting moment of what is quickly shaping up to be the best week of my life.

Because the week is ending.

I have more than enough money to leave Havensboro.

And I'm all too tempted to stay. At least until he leaves. And then follow him wherever he goes next, and—

I wake up the morning before his movie is due to start and realize, wrapped in his arms, that I love him.

Somewhere along the way, these past few days, I have indeed been wooed by him, falling headfirst into everything he's offering.

I sneak out of his arms, leaving him sleeping soundly, his head half-buried in pillows. We were up twice last night, both of us coming out of sleep to find ourselves tangled up, so desperately driven by this pull between us that we couldn't stay apart, not even in sleep.

The bathroom door groans as I shut it. I flick on my phone and pull up the email I've had saved for weeks, the one with the signed lease telling the apartment complex in Boston that I'm ready to make my deposit.

My finger hovers over the *Send* button.

I look up at my reflection in the mirror.

What do you want, Avery?

I want adventure. To get out of Havensboro and find life and chaos beyond these changeless shores.

Tom is that. He offers that and more, adoration and love and happiness unlike anything I could have hoped for.

But am I trading one island for another, in a way?

I want to leave Havensboro to find out who I am beyond these shores. Here, I'm forced to be a defined version of myself because of my job, my history, the way this island slots everyone into roles and never changes.

But if I let myself be swept away in Tom's life, what would that look like? Would I really be *me*, or would I become a different forced version of myself?

I look down at my phone.

My thumb hovers over the *Send* button. Slides to the *Delete* button. Back again.

Is it worth the risk?

Is *he* worth the risk?

CHAPTER NINE: TOM

The crew arrives in Havensboro, and immediately the mood of the island changes. I'm endlessly glad I opted to come early—there's no way I'd give the same performance without knowing how this island really is.

And then there's Avery, of course.

I still can't believe my luck. This week has been lifechanging in ways I never would have expected, and for once, I'm anxious for the shoot to end so I can get back to LA. I want her to come with me; I want to show her the house I rarely use and see if we can create a life there. Just the thought of building something with her has me grinning like a loon.

"You're different," Mark says to me. My manager's job is to note things like that, but it just makes me smile wider.

I cross my legs in the makeup chair and shrug. "Is that bad?"

"Nah, of course not. I think Jim's loving the new *lovesick* vibe you're giving off."

I look over my shoulder to where my agent is fast at work juggling the paparazzi who've crept onto Havensboro. The location helps keep this shoot more secluded, but a few of the more select sources have been allowed here. Jim has a clipboard in one hand as he balances the insistent questions of four people with cameras and recorders.

We just finished filming the first scene. The crew wasn't thrilled with the changes I'd insisted on making, but they acquiesced; or are still trying to, while we film the scenes that won't change with Maria's new bigger role.

"Are you ready?" Jim comes over to me. "They want a statement about the changes to the movie."

"Yep." I smile at the make-up artist, a tall blonde woman I've worked with before. "Thanks, Quinn."

She dabs my nose one more time, the diamond on her finger glinting in the sun. "Always a pleasure, sweetheart. Knock 'em dead."

But I'm staring at her hand.

A ring.

Of course.

That's what Avery deserves. A ring.
She isn't one for something huge, though. I
wonder if I'll be able to slip off the island and
find a jewelry store—

I glance around. There my darling is,
sitting on the sidewalk next to Gwen and
Kevin, the three of them laughing and
watching the crew scurry around Main Street.
It is quite a sight, and when
we're not shooting, the whole town has turned
up to gawk at the dozens of people needed to
make a film run. Even Ms. McDermott is
eyeing us from the porch of the Havensboro
Inn, and I think she's not even scowling.

I start to go to Avery, who meets my
eyes and smiles, and god help me, I want that
smile forever. Anxiety courses through me
now that I see her bare finger. I want my ring
there. I want her to know she's mine, and I'm
hers, and for the world to know we're one.

"Tom! Tom, over here." Jim grabs my
arm and swings me to the waiting interviews.

I give Avery a shrug and an apologetic
smile. She hesitates, sees the people waiting
to pepper me with questions, and waves it off.
But is that hurt on her face? I hate that for
even one second she'd feel hurt by this—

"Tom!" Jim pushes me. To the
paparazzi, he prods, "Go ahead."

CHAPTER TEN:
AVERY

I slip across the bustling street. The crew is setting up for the next scene and Tom is just near the diner, talking with a man he introduced as his agent, and a bunch of people with cameras. Doesn't take much of a guess to know who they are, and they lob questions at Tom as I come up behind him.

"...early, to learn as much as I could about the setting and character," Tom is saying.

One of the interviewers cuts him off to clarify something, and he smiles, cordial, ever the gentleman. The way he is with them is all professional, not a hint of resentment for how hard they must make his life or how many times he's done similar interviews before. He smiles, and thanks them, and listens intently.

They snap a dozen pictures of him as they talk. I hang back, arms crossed, lip caught between my teeth. I mean, can I blame them? He's stunning even dressed as Captain Small, an eighteenth-century costume that gives his whole physique a certain timelessness, as though he truly could have walked right off an old fishing boat.

He tosses his hair out of his face and catches me standing behind him. With a grin, he reaches for me, and that smile is one he doesn't use on anyone else. Just for me, private and sexy.

God help me, I love this man.

I love the way he loops his arm around my waist while he keeps taking questions.

I love the way he kisses my temple, strokes his thumb against my hip, letting me know he's fully aware that I'm here with him. He isn't afraid to let *them* know, either, and more pictures snap.

The questions turn to the rewrite of the script.

"She's actually to thank for that," Tom says and squeezes me to him. "This is Avery Watson. She helped me explore the true history of Havensboro."

One interviewer pulls the recorder to her own mouth and speaks low. "Tom Hudel's new girl is already affecting his career—what changes can we expect between this film and his last?"

Tom either didn't hear or ignores it; he nods at another interviewer who asks us to pose for a picture. The camera flashes, but I'm trying to listen to what they're saying to themselves, the notes they're taking.

Tom Hudel's new girl.

"Give me a second." I kiss his cheek—another picture.

"Not too long," he tells me and winks.

I slip away and pull my phone out. It doesn't take long to pull up a Google page featuring hit after hit, all about *Tom Hudel's new girl.*

I'm all over the internet already. Columns and forums and Tweets. I don't care about most of it—I really don't, internet trolls are trash—but as I scroll, something behind my ribs pinches.

I love him. I love him so much, so quickly, that I would willingly be *Tom Hudel's new girl.* I would go wherever he goes after this film and just…dissolve into him.

Is that what I want?

Yes, part of me says.

But another part, the part of me that's dreamed of getting out of Havensboro all my life, writhes. *No.*

My heart hammers, pulse too fast, too harsh.

This all happened so quickly. How did this happen so quickly?

I flip back to my email. Guilt spears through me when I see a reply. I haven't told Tom about it; I wasn't even sure why I'd sent in the deposit. I was—am?—so certain that I'll just go with him...

I look up to see Gwen and Kevin sitting on the sidewalk still, eyes on each other, totally content. They fit so well together because they'd both been absolutely sure of themselves when they'd met. They have a give-and-take, but one isn't dependent on the other.

And I am already so dependent on Tom.

My heart starts to crack when I look back at him, see him talking to his agent. He catches my eye, and smiles, and that crack breaks clean through.

I pull up that email again and open it.

It's the apartment complex in Boston confirming receipt.

I have a home waiting for me, one that's all mine, no strings attached as soon as I want it.

With the crew milling around the street, it's easy to slip over to Gwen.

She looks up at me, smiling, but immediately sobers when she sees the tears in my eyes. She rockets to her feet. "What's wrong?"

"I need to tell you something. And you can't judge me, all right? I just…need your help."

CHAPTER ELEVEN: TOM

Filming quickly consumes the rest of the day. And with my new hotel on the mainland, I hope Avery will invite me to stay at her place on Havensboro, but I can't find her after the scene wraps.

Most of the crew heads into the diner, and I follow. Avery isn't working tonight—I know her schedule—and when I text her, it goes unread.

Gwen, though, is at the counter, hastily serving the dozens of hungry crewmembers.

"Gwen!" I lean over the end.

She flurries past me, grabbing coffee pots.

"Gwen?" My voice rises.

Is she avoiding looking at me?

I move down the counter. Yep—she's definitely avoiding eye contact.

My pulse speeds up. Something's wrong.

I call Avery, but it rings and rings, then drops to voicemail.

A dark, riling thing in my chest pushes me behind the counter. A few of the crewmembers whoop, calling out orders to me in jest; but I stop right in Gwen's path.

"What happened?" I demand.

Gwen plants her hands on her hips. She has the iron-like expression that tells me she won't give away any details she doesn't want to, and that I'm in for a long night of fighting with her if I try.

But then she rolls her eyes. "You know what? She's being dumb. Go to her apartment. She's packing."

"What? Packing? Why?"

Someone calls for more coffee.

Gwen ignores them and bends closer to me, her face severe. "She's afraid of losing herself to you," she tells me, and my heart aches.

"Why would she—" I don't even have to finish the question. It's a fair concern. My life isn't exactly *small*, and could easily consume most people.

But Avery isn't most people.

And I wouldn't let her drown.

"Go talk to her," Gwen pushes me. "She's scared. And you're good for her. You'll give her the life she's searching for."

"I will." I plant a kiss on Gwen's forehead and she mock-swoons. Well, maybe not quite so *mock*—but she smiles at me, and I smile back.

The din of the diner immediately quiets when I get outside. The street is empty now, and I break into a run, bypassing the Inn, the few other quaint buildings on Main Street. The rest of Havensboro sits on unpaved roads that meander across the island, an island I've come to know so well now. It's stolen my heart entirely, much like the woman I'm running towards.

I cut across a lawn, through a small park; and there is Avery's apartment complex. She has one on the lower level, and I see the lights on within as she moves through her kitchen, throwing things into a bag, pausing occasionally to wipe the back of her hand across her nose.

My sweet, stubborn darling—why didn't she tell me what she was feeling?

But in the chaos that has been the past few days—the past *week*—I can't exactly fault her. Would I have wanted to damage the beauty we'd had? Would I have been able to interrupt the mad rush of my job, the demands, the insistency of my agent and manager?

That's what she needs to know, though. That no matter what I have going on, she comes first.

I stop in front of her door. I should knock; I'm shaking too hard, impatience and my own fear starting to creep up.

What if she does leave? What if I bear my soul to her, and she decides this life I have to offer isn't enough?

The door swings open with my fist still frozen midair.

"Tom," Avery gasps.

CHAPTER TWELVE: AVERY

"Tom," I say again, trying to fight against the tears building. Hell, I've been crying for hours, actually.

He isn't supposed to be here. I'm supposed to be on a ferry to the mainland before he realizes I'm gone, because if he *is* here, then I won't leave.

"Please," I hold up my hand when he opens his mouth to speak, "don't. Please just go. I need you to go."

"Why?" He steps forward, his face twisted up in agony. "You won't even speak to me? You would have snuck off and let me find out you'd gone through who—Gwen? The paparazzi?"

"No—I don't know!" I swing away, but he follows me into my apartment. I grab the bag half full of kitchen things and keep stuffing towels into it. "I need to do this. I can't...I don't know who I'd be with you. I need to find out who I *am*, Tom. People don't do this!"

"Do what?" He stands next to my table, watching me frantically pack, his arms slack, his eyebrows pinched, but overall, patient. He'd wait. He'd wait for me here; he'd wait for me later. God, he really would, wouldn't he?

"They don't fall in love with someone they just met!" I shout it at him, and tears fall again. "They don't uproot all their plans in the span of a week!"

Tom dashes around the table and takes my hands in his. "I would never ask you to give up your plans, darling. Tell me what you want. We'll make it work together."

"I want to go to Boston," I say, and god, I'm blubbering. "I want to be on my own, I want to find out who I am outside of Havensboro, I want—" I hiccup, and my hand lays flat on his chest, feeling the strong thud of his racing heart. He's as worked up as I am, but he's holding himself together. For me.

"I want you," I let myself admit, and I sob. "I want you so much it terrifies me. But I want other things, too, and I don't think it's possible to have—"

"Avery." Tom kisses my eyelid. "Avery, my darling, I would never ask you to lose yourself in my life. You want to live in Boston? Then you will live in Boston, and between my projects, I will make a home there too. I will visit you, and we will make love in your new apartment, and you will tell me all about what job you get, and we will both have our own lives that come together and build off of each other. I want you to stand on your own because you will be so very brilliant at whatever it is you do. I only ask that you let me bask in that brilliance. Please, let me be part of it."

"You...you're asking to be part of *my* life?" I gape up at him, and when he nods, I start crying helplessly, my head tipping to bow against his chest.

He wraps his arms around me, strong and secure. "Is that a yes?"

"Yes, it's a yes, oh my *god*." I surge up and kiss him, falling apart around him, messy tears and blotchy skin and desperate, painful kisses, but he holds me to him and catches me through all of it.

He lifts me up and swings me to sit on my kitchen counter. "There was one thing you said that I would like to revisit," he says, breathless.

"What?"

"That you fell in love with someone you just met?" His eyes sparkle. He kisses my top lip, my bottom lip. "I love you, Avery Watson. I—"

I kiss him silent. My heart is swelling, bursting with love for this man, and if he keeps speaking, I may just explode. "I love you too, Thomas Hudel."

He lifts my arms and pins them to the cupboards behind me, frantic kisses nipping down the side of my neck. He comes back up to my ear and licks the shell. "You scared me, darling. I think you owe me."

"Owe you?" Yes, I owe him. I—

He drops his hands from mine to rub his thumb at my clit through my jeans.

"Tom—"

"Give me this," he begs into my mouth. His fingers tug at the hem. "Pants off."

I nod, helpless, as always. But this time, I don't fight it; I'm swept up in him, utterly, viscerally.

I arch up to let him slip my pants off. The moment they hit the floor, he yanks my hips to the edge of the counter and plants his mouth on my pussy.

"Tom! Oh, fuck—" I writhe back. He's ruthless, his tongue diving into my folds and licking up to my slit in powerful, harsh strokes, punishing and devouring. I throw my head back and come embarrassingly fast, but that's what he does to me—rips me raw.

He rises up, his cock already out, and I nod, reaching for it, panting with need. No condom this time, neither of us hesitates— he's in me, pulling me off the counter to hold my body flush around his dick. Those lean, strong arms lift me, shove me down, rocking me on his cock with expert speed. I anchor around his neck and plant my heels against his ass but just let him use my body, an act of forgiveness for us both.

When he comes, I hold onto him, pinning him to me as he grunts and moans.

"I love you," I tell him.

Shuddering, he clamps his arms around me. "I love you," he says back.

We stumble through my small apartment to my bedroom and spend the rest of the night entwined in each other, making wordless plans for a future with room for two.

CHAPTER THIRTEEN: AVERY

Six Weeks Later

I check the clock on the stove again, for the hundredth time.

"He's not back yet?" Gwen asks from my phone. I have the screen propped up as I put the finishing touches on dinner.

"Any minute now. How do I look?" I step back so she can get a good look at my outfit, a simple black tank top tucked into a high-waisted slit skirt. I've even done up my hair and put on the necklace Tom got me after his *Run Aground* movie wrapped—a small anchor encrusted in diamonds.

"Gorgeous. He won't be able to resist," she tells me.

I roll my eyes and go back to cooking. "*That's* not the problem."

She snorts. "Then what is? You seem nervous."

"A little. I don't know. I—" I almost tell her. It just barely starts to slip out, but I bite down at the last second. He needs to know first. Not that I don't trust Gwen not to keep it to herself, it's just…

He needs to know first.

The door rattles.

"He's here!" I chirp, maybe a little too loudly. "Gotta go. Call you later?"

Gwen gives me an odd look. A slow smile spreads across her face. "Avery. Oh my god. Are you—"

"*Bye*, Gwen, I love you." I hang up on her open mouth.

The door swings open, giving me no time to dwell on the ball of anxiety in my stomach. Tom steps inside, his eyes going straight to me, in the kitchen.

He drops his bag, shuts the door, and races across the room. I'm halfway too him, and I jump up, letting him catch me midair.

It's only been a month and a half since I officially moved off Havensboro. He's been in LA for the past two weeks, getting his house sold there and starting on preliminary plans for another film; *Run Aground* wrapped three weeks ago, which meant we only saw each other for a too-short week in between. I love my independence here, but I also hate any moment that's not right *here*, in his arms.

Tom spins me around. "God, I missed you, darling." He stops and smells the air. His face widens in a smile. "Pancakes?"

"The Havensboro Diner recipe," I tell him and wiggle against him. "Put me down! They're burning."

"The worst thing you can ask of me— to choose between your body and *pancakes*." But he relents and I rush back to the kitchen to take the last batch off the griddle just in time.

Tom comes up behind me and gently bites my exposed neck. "A fancy meal, a fancy, sexy outfit—all this to celebrate my homecoming? Or are you trying to convince me that we don't *need* a full wedding again?"

I whirl and thread my arms around his neck. My engagement ring catches the light, a small, tasteful diamond that never fails to melt my heart.

"I *will* convince you to at least scale back the size of the wedding—"

"Ha!"

"—but no, that's not what this dinner is for." Nerves catch up to me, make my whole body tremble in a sudden wave.

Tom feels it. His face gets severe, teasing gone. "Avery? What's wrong?"

I lick my lips. His eyes don't even drop there, totally focused on me, and it's only because of that intent that I'm able to say the words.

"I'm pregnant."

There's a pause. I see the information sink into him.

Then he seizes me, hugging me to him. "Oh my god, darling—are you sure?"

"Yes! Yes." I'm laughing, and he is too. He pulls back and there are tears in his eyes when I cup his jaw in my hand. "I've taken a dozen tests. It's real."

"Darling." Tom kisses me, his tongue gliding into my mouth, and we don't need to say anything else. I can feel his happiness as strongly as I feel my own.

Tom starts to back us up towards the hall. "Dinner will wait. I need to eat something else first."

I giggle.

But I plant my feet, stopping him. "Wait! Wait—"

I swing open the fridge and pull out a cannister of whipped cream.

Tom throws his head back with a laugh. When he looks at me again, his eyes are all pupil, feral and hungry. "Such a tease, darling."

He grabs my wrist and I squeal with joy as he lifts me into his arms and carries me into our bedroom.

I left Havensboro for independence. To figure out who I am on my own. Getting pregnant will be decidedly the *least* alone thing I ever do, but there's a sense of peace about it.

This is meant to be. Me with Tom, and now, our little family.

THE END

For more sizzling celebrity fantasies brought to life, check out the next two books in the *Celebrity Crush* series:

PLOT TWIST: A makeup artist breaks her no-dating-celebrities rule when the newest hot shot leading man, Sebastian Lanik, finds himself in her chair. But what happens when a little bit of fun turns a little too serious?

OFF CAMERA: A PR intern accepts an unorthodox assignment to be Hollywood bad boy Chris Griffin's faux-girlfriend—and gets far more than she bargained for…

Stay up-to-date on any releases from Natasha Luxe, join her shared newsletter with Liza Penn!

You'll get double the spicy reads for one easy sign up. (But don't worry, we won't spam you—max two emails a month!)

https://rarebooks.substack.com/welcome

Read on for
an exclusive excerpt
from Celebrity Crush:
PLOT TWIST!

The beat rises. I don't recognize the song, but I make a mental note to ask the DJ for a set list later—I'm definitely adding this to my regulars. Maybe to my workout playlists. Or my sex playlists. Because, yeah, you gotta have at least one sex playlist, right? And the way this girl loops her arms around my neck as we jump with the crowd, swept up into the chaos whether we want to go or not—this song is all sex.

So is she.

Her tight little body is barely contained in the black dress she's wearing, her breasts swelling against the low neckline, the hem wrapped around the barest top of her thighs. All she'd have to do is bend over, and I could—

She spins around, pressing her ass back into my crotch. I'm hard—I've been hard since she touched my wrist—and I know she feels it. My hands stay on her waist, sliding around to cup her belly, and I try, really, I do, to not reach too low, but then she jumps again, and my fingers brush her pussy through her dress.

I jump, too, because if I don't, I'll blow my load right then. The way this girl moves, every muscle in her body strung taut, her face relaxed in total euphoria, her curves hitting the beats and her limbs arching seductively—she has me on edge in every way.

She leans back into me, her head falling over my shoulder, exposing her long neck.

My lips go to that skin, sweat-slick and glistening, and *Christ*, nothing has ever tasted so perfect. She's wearing some kind of vanilla perfume that shoots straight to my throbbing cock. Where else does she smell like this? Between her breasts? Her slit? Fuck, fuck—

Her body goes stiff momentarily, and I freeze too—I fucked up. This went too far. Shit.

But then she rocks her hips back into my hard-on again. One of her hands reaches down, takes my wrist, and lifts it to palm her breast.

I hiss and my hand flexes on her boob, feeling her hard, pebbled nipple through the slinky fabric.

My lips climb to her ear. "Careful, doll. You're playing with fire."

Her lips curve into a grin that catches in a beam of blue light.

She spins again, coming face to face, and she kisses me right there on the dance floor. We may as well be alone, though—everyone is so wrapped up in their own dancing that two people making out is hardly exciting. Her tongue darts into my mouth and I moan against it, cradling the back of her head to go deeper, deeper. She returns with her own enthusiasm, one leg arching up to wrap around my thighs, pressing the heat of her pussy right over my erection.

Is she wearing panties?

Christ.

She spins again, and I'm left in a stumbling haze of painful arousal and downright aching confusion. I don't even know this girl. What the *fuck*. What the—

Her ass is against my crotch again. The music carries on, but suddenly the only thing I'm aware of is the way she's slowly pulling up the back of her dress.

I suck in a breath and plant my fingers into her hips. "What are you doing?" I growl into her ear.

She keeps going until her ass is bare, protected only by my crotch.

Then her fingers fumble at my belt buckle.

"Christ, doll—"

"Afraid to get caught?" She glances back at me with a grin so downright sexy, so tempting, that any rational thought is long dead.

She. Wants me to fuck her. On the dance floor. Surrounded by dozens of people.

Oh my god.

Oh my *god*.

Her fingers work behind her back, undoing my belt, my fly. She reaches in, but I bat her fingers aside and work myself free as discreetly as I can. The darkness creates a cocoon around us, the press of bodies might as well be walls; so when I pull my dick out of my pants, it doesn't feel like I'm doing it in public.

Thank god I always have a condom in my pocket. This is why. This is absolutely why.

I roll it on as I slide my other hand down her ass, finding her slit by feel. She's hot, scorching hot, and her tight folds close around my fingers, squeezing hard. My dick is wet with pre-cum—I need to be inside her, need it *now*.

While I work for the best angle, I loop my arm around her front and slip my fingers up under her dress. Her clit is swollen already and when I touch it, she throws her head back against my shoulder, her body limp, mine for the taking.

My cock finds her entrance.

The music rises, rises—

When it breaks, the dancers scream, and I shove into her. The girl cries out, her pleasure lost in the masses. The beat sets off thumping, and I move in time with it.

She's so fucking tight. The walls of her pussy contract around me as I bounce into her, electric sensations flitting into my balls, begging for release. But I refuse to go until she does, until she screams out into the club.

My fingers work that clit, rubbing in gentle, smooth circles that follow the sway of the music. I want my tongue there; I want to taste her; I settle for licking her neck, biting her earlobe, sucking it into my mouth.

"This is what I'll be doing to that hot little clit of yours," I say into her ear. "I'm going to get you some place where I can fuck you properly. You like my cock inside you?"

I thrust, and she nods, her eyelids fluttering, her face contorted in the building ecstasy of impending orgasm.

"I'm gonna come," she gasps, and I barely just read the words on her lips. "I'm gonna—"

I take her clit between my thumb and finger, and I pinch it.

She screams. The music swells, swallowing it, and I follow her over the edge, cursing into her neck as my dick unloads inside her, balls squeezing tight. I brace her hips and rock hard into her, and she cries out again, those tight muscles shuddering around my cock.

We come down from it together, swaying gently, though the music is still rough and fast.

She's the one who pulls herself together first. She eases forward and slides her dress back into place. I grab my dick and stuff it back into my pants, condom and all. But she doesn't go far; she twists, wrapping her arms around my neck, and then her mouth is on mine again, a slower, luxurious kiss as she traces my jaw with her thumb.

Oh my god. Who the fuck is this girl? I'm in love. There's no other word for it. I'd punch out a hundred creeps for her; I'd follow her to the ends of the earth.

"Your name," I mumble into her mouth. "Your number. I need to see you again."

She grins. Did she hear me? Fuck this music.

I bend to her ear. "I need to see you again."

She kisses my neck and mimes getting a drink. She wants a drink? I'll get her one of everything at this bar.

But when I start after her, she waves me off. "I'll be back," she mouths.

I don't want her out of my sight.

Her eyes drop to my crotch. Oh. Yeah. I should probably take care of that.

I point toward the bathrooms. She nods, and bites her lip in a grin, and oh my god, yep, I'm in love.

I race through the crowd and clean up in the bathroom in two seconds flat. My heart thunders, or maybe it's the music, or maybe it's my body realizing I just fucked the most gorgeous girl on a dance floor, and this is it, this is the pinnacle of happiness.

Back out on the main floor, I hurry to the bar.

The only people there are a few couples, one lone guy.

I scan the area. Elbows like battering rams, I dive into the dancers, but none are *her*, that bright hair, that lithe body.

When I stumble out by the entrance, my heart sinks into my toes.

She's gone.

Made in the USA
Las Vegas, NV
21 October 2021